Archie and the Bear

For Rosie, in her bear suit —**Z.L.**

For William Venturini, the capo —**D.M.**

Clarion Books
3 Park Avenue
New York, New York 10016

Text copyright © 2017 by Zanni Louise
Illustrations copyright © 2017 by David Mackintosh
First published in Australia in 2017 by Little Hare Books,
an imprint of Hardie Grant Egmont.
First U.S. edition, 2018.

Clarion Books is an imprint of Houghton Mifflin
Harcourt Publishing Company.

hmco.com

The illustrations in this book were made using pen,
pencil, ink, watercolor, and kraft paper.
The text was set in Sentinel.
Designed and hand-lettered by David Mackintosh

Library of Congress Cataloging-in-Publication Data
Names: Louise, Zanni, author. | Mackintosh, David
(Illustrator), illustrator.
Title: Archie and the bear / Zanni Louise, David Mackintosh.
Description: First U.S. edition. | Boston ; New York : Clarion
Books, Houghton Mifflin Harcourt, 2018. | "First published in
Australia in 2017 by Little Hare Books, an imprint of Hardie
Grant Egmont." | Summary: "Archie is a bear, not a boy in a
bear suit. He meets a bear, who claims to be a boy, not a bear in
a boy suit. The two spend the day together, teaching each other
about being bears and being boys—pretend or otherwise"—
Provided by publisher.
Identifiers: LCCN 2017028919 | ISBN 9781328973412
(hardcover)
Subjects: | CYAC: Bears—Fiction. | Imagination—Fiction. |
Human-animal relationships—Fiction.
Classification: LCC PZ7.1.L72 Arc 2018 | DDC [E]—dc23
LC record available at https://lccn.loc.gov/2017028919

Manufactured in China
ECB 10 9 8 7 6 5 4 3 2 1
4500684998

Archie and the Bear

zanni louise
david mackintosh

Clarion Books

Houghton Mifflin Harcourt
Boston   New York

Archie was a bear.

But everywhere Archie went, people
patted him on the head and said,
"I like your bear suit."

"It's NOT a suit," Archie would growl. "I AM a bear!"

One day, Archie had had enough.
He packed his bear sack
and set off for the forest.

Archie walked and stumbled
and walked.

He rested against a tree
and nibbled his honey sandwich.

By afternoon,
the forest
had begun to
grow dark.

Archie knew
bears shouldn't
be scared, so he
kept walking
and sharpened
his bear eyes.

Just then,
a bear appeared.

"Argh!"
cried
Archie.

"Hello," said the bear.

When Archie realized the
bear was friendly, he said,
"I like your boy suit."

"It's NOT a suit," growled the bear. "I AM a boy!"

The bear was clearly not a boy.
But Archie didn't want to hurt the
bear's feelings.

"Would you like a
honey sandwich?"
asked Archie.

The bear smiled and took a bite.

"Boys like sandwiches," he said.

"Bears like honey,"
said Archie.

Archie and the bear walked along the river.

The bear showed Archie how to skim stones across the water.

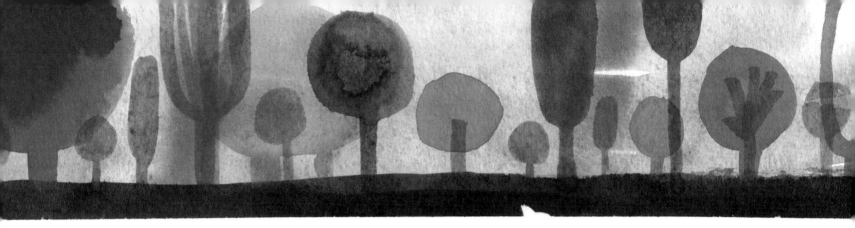

Archie was very good at skimming stones.

Archie showed the bear how
to catch fish with his claw.

The bear was very
good at catching fish.

The bear showed
Archie how to read.

Archie read to the bear.

Archie showed the bear how to
scoop honey from the log.

The bear scooped
honey out for Archie.

As night
deepened,
the forest
cooled.

The bear
shivered.

"Would you like to wear my
bear suit?" asked Archie.
"Yes, please," said the bear.

Archie undressed.
Then he too shivered.

The bear took off his boy sweater
and gave it to Archie.
But still, they were cold.

"Do boys like warm quilts?" asked
Archie. "I have a very warm one
where I live."

The bear nodded,
so Archie led the bear home.

At home, a fire burned.
They nibbled honey sandwiches
until the shivering stopped.

They pulled the warm quilt around them.

"Boys like warm quilts, warm fires, and honey sandwiches," said the bear.

"So do bears," said Archie.